*News*paper Hats

To Fa Fa, Nanna Luce and our newspaper hats. xxx — PC

To Pop — OS

Scholastic Press
An imprint of Scholastic Australia Pty Limited (ABN 11 000 614 577)
PO Box 579 Gosford NSW 2250
www.scholastic.com.au

Part of the Scholastic Group
Sydney • Auckland • New York • Toronto • London • Mexico City
• New Delhi • Hong Kong • Buenos Aires • Puerto Rico

First published by Scholastic Australia in 2015.
This edition published in 2024.

NATIONAL LIBRARY OF AUSTRALIA
A catalogue record for this book is available from the National Library of Australia

ISBN: 978-1-76152-081-5

Typeset in Granjon.

Owen Swan used watercolour and pencil on paper to create this artwork.

Printed in China by RR Donnelley.
Scholastic Australia's policy, in association with RR Donnelley, is to use papers that are renewable and made efficiently with wood from responsibly managed sources, so as to minimise its environmental footprint.

10 9 8 7 6 5 4 3 2 1 24 25 26 27 28 / 2

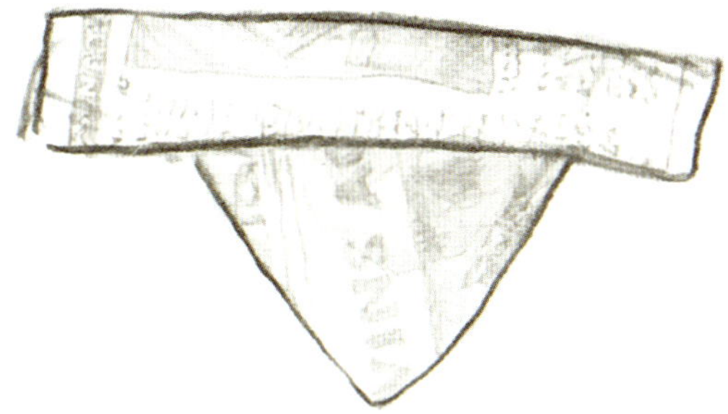

*News*paper Hats

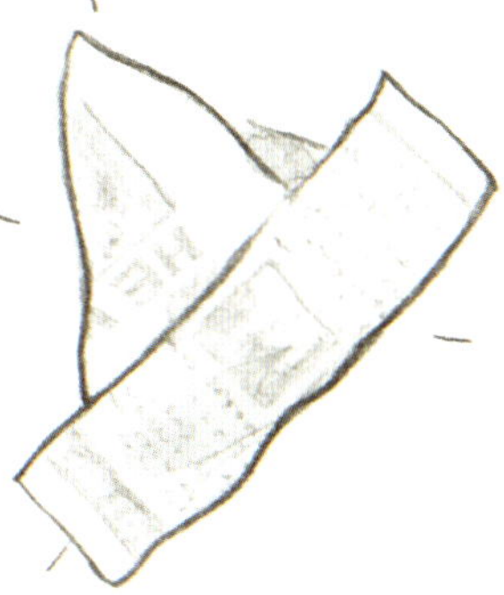

Phil Cummings

Owen Swan

A Scholastic Press book from Scholastic Australia

Georgie walked through the doors that opened like curtains.

‘Will Grandpa remember me today?’ she asked.
Her father squeezed her hand and smiled. ‘Wait and see.’

They walked down
corridors that twisted
and turned . . .

until they came to a sky-blue door.

Grandpa's room was full of sunshine.
His collection of old newspapers were stacked
around him like tall city buildings.

'Hi, Grandpa,' said Georgie.

Grandpa put his newspaper down.
He looked into Georgie's wide eyes.
'Hello there,' was all he said.

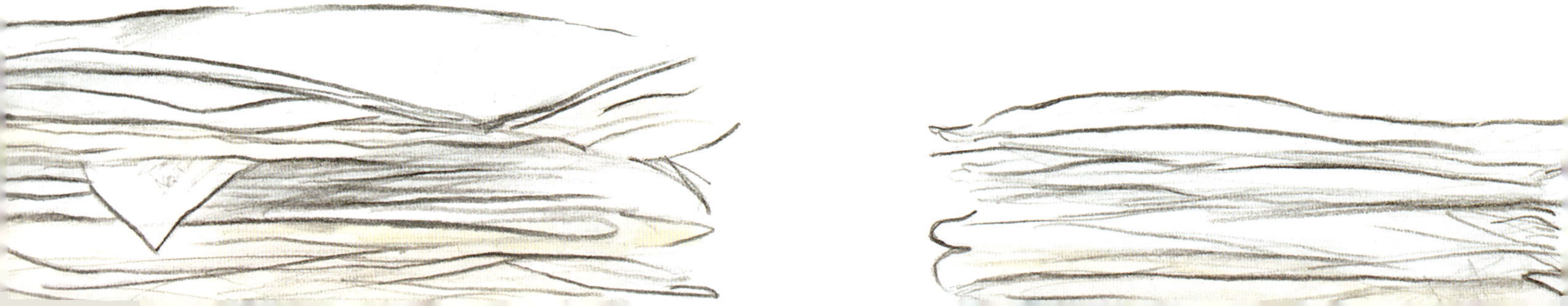

'Grandpa,' said Georgie, 'do you remember me?'

Grandpa looked away and reached for a photo on the shelf. 'I remember my brother, and tadpoles in tins,' he said. 'And summer rain from thunderclouds that tasted like dust.'

'I love the rain in summer,' said Georgie.

'But do you remember me ?'

‘I remember my mum in the kitchen,’ said Grandpa. ‘The fire was warm. She baked crusty bread and spread it with butter and honey. The honey melted all over my fingers.’

‘I love honey on warm bread, too,’ said Georgie.

'But Grandpa, do you remember me?'

‘The rain was hard in the jungle. The chopper blades sliced the air and wild wind whipped through the trees. I was frightened.’

Georgie squeezed Grandpa.
'Don't be frightened, Grandpa.'

'Here,' said Georgie. 'That's me, that's you and that's Dad. You made me a newspaper hat, remember?'

Grandpa smiled. 'I love newspaper hats,' he said.

'So do I,' said Dad.

'Me too,' said Georgie. 'Let's make them now.'

Flip . . .

Flap . . .

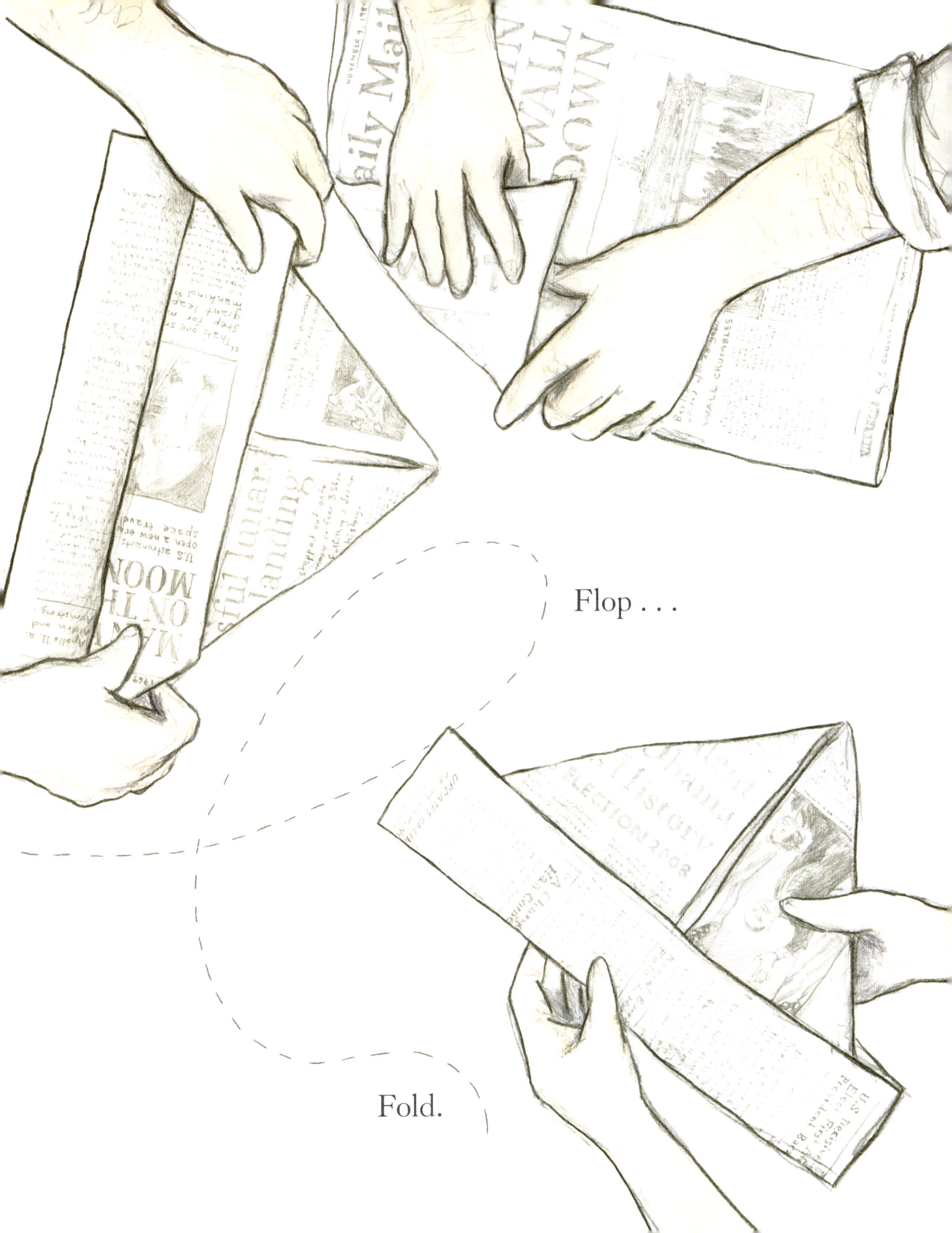

Flop . . .

Fold.

When the hats were finished, they walked out into the garden.

Georgie helped Grandpa give hats to his friends.

Mary sang.

Big Bruno clapped.

And the baby bouncing on
Mrs Carlton's lap giggled.

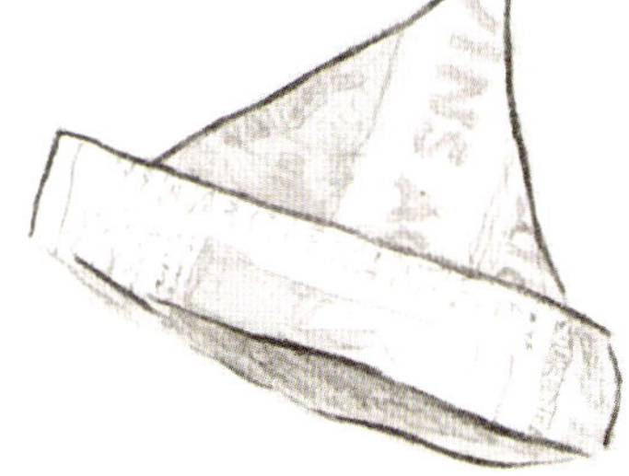

Suddenly, a gust of wind lifted Grandpa's hat and swept it away.

'I'll get it!' Georgie cried.

She jumped,

she twirled,

she skipped,

she ran.

But she couldn't catch it.

'Don't worry, Grandpa,' said Georgie.
'We can make another one.'
'Yes,' said Grandpa. 'I remember how.'